Beatrice Zinker

UPSIDE DOWN THINKER

For Stephen Barr—
in glittering gold

Copyright © 2017 by Shelley Johannes

All rights reserved. Published by Disney • Hyperion, an imprint of Disney Book Group.
No part of this book may be reproduced or transmitted in any form or by any means,
electronic or mechanical, including photocopying, recording, or by any information storage
and retrieval system, without written permission from the publisher. For information
address Disney • Hyperion, 125 West End Avenue, New York, New York 10023.
First Hardcover Edition, September 2017
First Paperback Edition, April 2018
3 5 7 9 10 8 6 4 2
FAC-020093-18163

Printed in the United States of America

This book is set in Amsterdamer Garamont Pro/Fontspring
Designed by Phil Caminiti and Shelley Johannes
Illustrations created with felt-tip pen, brush marker, and colored pencil on tracing paper

Library of Congress Cataloging-in-Publication Control
Number for Hardcover Edition: 2016054238
ISBN 978-1-4847-6814-3
Visit www.DisneyBooks.com

THIS LABEL APPLIES TO TEXT STOCK

Beatrice Zinker

UPSIDE DOWN THINKER

by Shelley Johannes

DISNEP • HYPERION

LOS ANGELES   NEW YORK

1
THE VERY BEGINNING

Beatrice Zinker always did her best thinking
upside down. It worked like magic,
and she never questioned it.

It worked like poof.
It worked like presto.
It worked like shazam—
on every problem,
every pickle, and
each and every jam.

But not everything in her life was a piece of cake.

The Zinkers were a right-side-up family.

Being the upside down daughter wasn't easy.

KATE   BEATRICE   HENRY

Her siblings didn't make things any easier. Beatrice was the middle child. Her older sister, Kate, was a cookie-cutter version of their mother, Nancy. Her baby brother, Henry, was a cookie-cutter version of their father, Pete. Even the cat seemed cut out to be a Zinker.

PINEAPPLE UPSIDE DOWN CAKE

Beatrice, however, had been different from the very beginning.

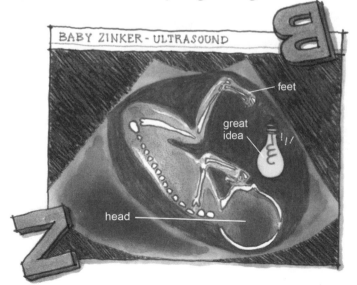

BABY ZINKER - ULTRASOUND

feet

great idea

head

The Zinkers liked boxes
and boundaries.

But not Beatrice.

She climbed out of her first
box as soon as she was able.

Kate's first word was MOM.
When Beatrice finally spoke,
her first word was WOW.

"Wow, indeed," said
her father.
"Uh-oh," said Kate.

"Oh no," said her mother, "what now?"

As Beatrice grew, Kate said a lot of UH-OH.
Nancy Zinker said a lot of OH NO and a lot of
WHAT NOW?

When Beatrice was five years old, she headed off to William Charles Elementary. It was an upstanding institution with a stand-up reputation.

"Keep your chin up, buttercup," encouraged her father.

"Take it easy on Mrs. Beasley," her mother teased.

Beatrice tried her best.

She filled up on facts and figures five days a week. She sat at circle time. She relied on the rules and relaxed into the routine.

But kindergarten couldn't counteract the pull of gravity. Despite a daily dose of ABCs and 123s, her mind still gravitated toward MAYBES, WHAT-IFS, and COULD-BES.

"Maybe she'll outgrow it," said the parents at pickup time.

"Maybe . . ." said Nancy Zinker.

MAYBE was actually one of Beatrice's
favorite words.

Occasionally one
of her MAYBEs was
a hit.

And others saw things her way.

It didn't happen often.
Nothing happened fast.

But in first grade—
on Halloween night, to be exact—
Beatrice found a friend named Lenny.
In matching costumes, they found
plenty of candy

and lots of common ground.

After that they
spent recess in
the trees,

sailing
high seas, and
fending off
zombies.

Sometimes they were ninjas.
Some days they were knights.
Each day their high kicks and
hijinks reached brave new heights.

In the eyes of Lenny Santos, Beatrice was not a problem to be solved—she was the perfect partner in crime.

By second grade, even her teacher came around.

At the graduation ceremony that spring, the whole class filed into the gym. Mrs. Walker crossed the stage and faced the crowd. Holding a piece of paper and a microphone, she asked Beatrice to join her.

"This year, Beatrice reminded me that there are infinite upsides to being yourself. Infinite upsides, and infinite upside down sides, too." Beatrice squinted under the lights as Mrs. Walker made it official. "This special award goes to Beatrice Zinker—our very own, very best Upside Down Thinker."

"Wow," said Beatrice.

"Wow, indeed," said her father from the second row.

Her mother stood up to snap a picture and spotted a problem.

The award was upside down.

"Flip it around," she told Beatrice.

Beatrice turned the paper right side up and struck a picture-perfect pose.

"TA-DA!" she said.

Once she had it in writing,
there was no turning back.

2
LOOK OUT, WORLD!

Every idea starts as a tiny seed—even the biggest idea of the very best upside down thinker. Three months later, Beatrice launched the most important plan of her upside down life, but the seed of the idea was planted that very afternoon in June, on graduation day.

The award was still crisp in her hands.

The ink was still damp.

Her cheeks still hurt from smiling.

Beatrice had never felt better.

After the ceremony, everyone poured onto the playground for a picnic. Lenny found Beatrice hanging out in her favorite spot. "You've got that look on your face again," Lenny said. "The one that always gets you into trouble."

"I know," said Beatrice, "but today it got me this."

Lenny held up two dripping waffle cones. "I brought ice cream," she said. "To celebrate." She lifted up one of the cones like a microphone. "Beatrice Zinker, can you tell the audience what it feels like to be an award winner?"

Beatrice accepted the mic. "It feels really good," she said. "Like I'm finally free to be me."

"Look out, world!" Lenny shouted into her ice cream. "Beatrice is on the loose!"

"Shhh!" said Beatrice. "People might get suspicious." She lowered her voice and looked around. "The best plan I've ever had just popped into my head, but in order for it to work, it has to stay a secret."

BEATRICE is ON THE LOOSE!

"Hurry up and tell me!" said Lenny. "I love secrets."

Lenny covered her
microphone, and
Beatrice laid out
her latest plan.

"Whoa," said Lenny. Her eyes twinkled behind her glasses. "Next year just got interesting." She leaned against the tree and took a bite of her ice cream. "Do we get to have a secret base?"

"Yep—and we'll need to do a lot of reconnaissance."

"What's reconnaissance?"

"Spying," Beatrice said. "People aren't always who they appear to be . . . especially when they know someone's watching."

Lenny nodded her head and leaned in. "I've always wanted a good reason to be a spy."

"Me too." Beatrice licked her ice cream casually, like they were discussing their upcoming summer vacations and not masterminding a mission. "Do you still have your ninja suit?"

"Of course," said Lenny. "I'm never getting rid of that thing. You can get away with a lot in a ninja suit."

"That's what I'm counting on," said Beatrice. "So you're in?"

"Of course! If I wasn't so excited to see my cousins, I'd skip my trip and get right to third grade."

Beatrice faltered. "I forgot about your trip."

Lenny's family was spending the summer in the Philippines. Two drops of ice cream dripped from Beatrice's cone into the grass, just missing Lenny's shoelaces.

Drip. Drop.

It was hard to imagine those same feet would be standing on the other side of the world in a few days.

"When do you get back?"

Lenny shrugged. "Sometime before school starts?"

"Well," said Beatrice, "at least we have something to look forward to. On our first day back, we'll dress in black and the fun begins."

"Deal," said Lenny, tapping Beatrice's half-eaten cone with her own. "Here's to really good secrets—and all the upsides of you being you."

3
THE FIRST DAY BACK

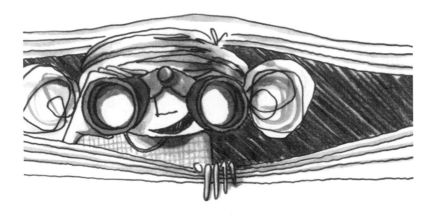

While Lenny was away, Beatrice spent her summer practicing ninja moves and brainstorming names for their secret operation. When the first day of school finally arrived, Beatrice woke up smiling.

She lifted the blinds and confirmed what she already knew to be true. It was going to be a good day. The sun was shining. Birds were chirping. Best of all, Mrs. Jenkins was walking her cat. Good things always happened when Mrs. Jenkins walked Scrappy.

Operation Upside was destined for success.

Beatrice rolled over in her bunk and got to work. She tugged her black turtleneck over her head. She pulled on her black pants. Once she was in uniform, she flipped over the rail and scaled down the side of her bed.

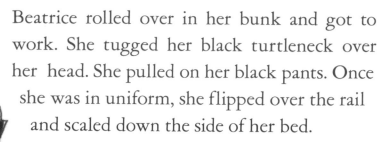

Her sister, Kate, stood in a sunny square in the middle of the room, smoothing the wrinkles in her cardigan. She glanced up at Beatrice. "There is no way Mom is going to let you go to school in that." "Why not?" said Beatrice. "It's my favorite outfit." She had high hopes for the day. All of them involved her ninja suit. "You look like a criminal." "No, I don't," Beatrice replied. "I look like me."

She had lived in her ninja suit all summer. She only wore something else on laundry days, or when her mother made her.

"*Excusez-moi*," said Kate, who was on a foreign-language kick, "I'm just trying to help."

"Maybe she won't even notice," said Beatrice.

Kate raised an eyebrow. When it came to Beatrice, Nancy Zinker noticed everything.

"Just don't say anything," Beatrice suggested. "And if you really can't help yourself, say it in French, so she has no idea what you're saying."

"All I'm saying is, I would have a backup plan if I were you."

Kate pointed at the dress their mother left out for Beatrice. "Like that."

PINK
PINK
PINK
PINK

Beatrice wrinkled her nose. Nothing said I HAVE ABSOLUTELY NO INTENTION OF THINKING UPSIDE DOWN TODAY like a pink, flowery dress.

And today—the day she would finally see Lenny again—Beatrice was full of upside down intention.

Kate had a point, though. She did need a plan.

Just not the kind of plan that involved a dress, or anything pink, or anything floral.

Beatrice yanked open her closet door and turned to Kate. "Tell Mom that I'll be down in a minute."

4
BEATRICE'S PLAN

There were few things Nancy Zinker hated more than her daughter's ninja suit. Beatrice's plan revolved around all three of them.

A black mask concealed her face.

A striped hat covered her head.

Long black gloves stretched over her elbows.

Beatrice took a deep breath and walked into the kitchen.

Morning activity stopped.

"Uh-oh," said Kate.

"Oh no," said Nancy Zinker, spinning away from the counter with a jar of peanut butter in one hand and a knife in the other. "What now?"

Pete Zinker folded down a corner of his newspaper. Henry peeked over the top of his yogurt cup. Oliver, the family cat, hid behind the high chair.

"Wow," Beatrice said. "It smells really good in here."

"It's the bacon," said her father, holding up the evidence. Bacon was his breakfast specialty.

Nancy Zinker ignored the bacon. "You are not wearing that to school, Beatrice," she said.

"I told you," mouthed Kate.

"You look like a criminal," said her mother.

"That's what I said," whispered Kate.

Nancy Zinker set the jar on the counter and balanced the knife on its rim. She held out her hand. "Hand over the mask," she said.

Beatrice reached behind her head and loosened the ties. She surrendered the black fabric to her mother. Nancy Zinker wiggled her fingers.

"The gloves, too."

Beatrice tugged off the gloves.

"And the hat."

"My thinking cap?"

"We do not have time to argue about this, Beatrice."

Beatrice pulled off the hat and handed it over.

Mother and daughter stood toe-to-toe. The mask was missing. The hat was off. The gloves were gone.

But Beatrice was still wearing the ninja suit.

Nancy Zinker reached out and smoothed Beatrice's flyaway hairs. "Much better," she said.

Beatrice held her breath and waited.

"Now hurry up and eat your breakfast. You need your protein. The bus will be here any second."

Nancy Zinker went back to the counter, scrambling to finish their lunches. Pete Zinker winked and went back to his reading. Henry returned to his yogurt.

Kate, for once, was speechless.

Beatrice took her place at the table and tried not to smile. Everything had gone exactly as planned.

Kate flipped a flash card at her.

Her father slipped her an extra piece of bacon.

With her heart thudding in her chest, Beatrice kept a straight face. It was too soon to celebrate. She wasn't out of the woods until she was out of the house.

The ninja suit still had to survive breakfast.

5

EAKFAST-BRAY

Breakfast went like most meals in the Zinker household. Henry was the star of the show.

Beatrice crunched her bacon and waited for it to begin. It didn't take long.

Henry drained the last of his yogurt and thunked the empty container on his tray.

Every head turned toward the high chair.

Pete Zinker folded his paper in his lap. "Did you hear that, honey?" he asked.

Nancy Zinker clapped her hands. "He said, 'More, please!'"

Kate threw her flash cards on the table. "In Swahili!"

Pete grabbed Henry another yogurt while Nancy dashed for the camera.

Pete Zinker ruffled Henry's fuzzy head. "Atta boy, buddy," he said. Kate scooted her chair over to her brother and flipped through her flash cards.

Kate dabbled in a dozen languages. Henry was a baby genius.

Beatrice spoke Pig Latin. (Her talent was generally underappreciated.)

"*An-cay ou-yay ass-pay e-thay yrup-say ease-play?*" she asked.

"*Pardon?*" said Kate.

"What?" her parents asked in unison.

"*Ga?*" said Henry, possibly in Gaelic.

Kate pointed at Henry. "Did you hear that?"

Nancy Zinker snapped another picture. "I sure did!"

No one passed the syrup.

Beatrice shrugged and stretched across the table. *"Evermind-nay,"* she said and grabbed it herself.

"Mind your manners, Beatrice," said her mother. "It's not polite to reach." She stood behind Henry to get a better view and refocused her camera. "Pete, did you see his tray? It's my favorite yet."

HENRY ZINKER
MIXED MEDIA

Moments later, the familiar squeal of hydraulic brakes interrupted the show.

"Bus!" Nancy Zinker called out.

Beatrice shoveled in a final bite of breakfast, then hopped to her feet. Her ninja suit was one step closer to safety.

Kate ran out the door shouting *"Au revoir!"* while Beatrice hurried to keep up. The bus waited at the corner with its red lights flashing.

Beatrice was halfway down the concrete steps, about to jump to the sidewalk, when Pete Zinker stepped onto the porch, his newspaper rolled into a megaphone.

"Hey, B?" he called to her.

Beatrice turned around. The bus doors were already opening for Kate.

She was so close.

"Keep your chin up, buttercup," he said with a smile. He said the same thing every day. By now Beatrice knew what he really meant. It was simultaneous dad code for "I love you!" and "Please, for the love of Pete—stay right side up today."

Beatrice flashed her dad a thumbs-up before

jogging toward the waiting bus. She hoped he wouldn't misinterpret the gesture as any sort of agreement.

NOT A PROMISE →

Today was not a day for right-side-up promises. She'd waited all summer for this moment.

Operation Upside was a go, and she and Lenny Santos had big plans.

6

RIGHT ON CUE

Classroom 3B swarmed with familiar
faces and new backpacks. But there
was only one person Beatrice
wanted to find. Standing in the
middle of the room, Beatrice
spun in a full circle, checking
every face. She didn't see
Lenny anywhere.

"You must be
Beatrice," said a
voice behind her.

Beatrice turned to find Mrs. Tamarack, her new teacher. Evelyn Tamarack was a legend at William Charles Elementary. She put the upstanding in the school's stand-up reputation.

Beatrice held out her hand and introduced herself. "Beatrice Zinker," she said. "Upside down thinker."

"I am well aware, Miss Zinker," Mrs. Tamarack informed her.

Beatrice tried to concentrate on her new teacher, but Lenny was missing. Her eyes drifted to the door.

Lots of kids came in—Operation Upside would never run out of candidates to spy on—but no Lenny.

NOT LENNY.   NOT LENNY.   NOPE.

AND, NO.   NO ONE...   STILL NO.

Mrs. Tamarack cleared her throat.

"You should know," she told Beatrice, "I am not like your other teachers. I do not give awards for bad behavior. And I do not tolerate upside down antics in my classroom." Three more kids came in the door. "But if you save your tricks for outdoors," said Mrs. Tamarack, "I believe we'll get along just fine."

Beatrice earnestly nodded her head. "I will try my best."

"You'll get three reminders—then recess is on the line."

The door swung open again. Always-tardy Sam Darzi slipped into the room—but still no Lenny.

"Don't worry," said Beatrice. "Recess is very important to me. Especially this year." Operation Upside would take every spare moment and more.

Mrs. Tamarack let out her breath. "That's very good to hear."

Right on cue, Lenny Santos walked through the door.

7

IMPOSTOR!

At least someone who looked a lot like Lenny walked through the door.

Beatrice had known Lenny Santos since she was six years old. She would recognize her anywhere. Lenny's hair was short and shaggy. Lenny wore bright green glasses. She loved her brother's hand-me-downs and lived for adventure.

The girl in the doorway was not quite Lenny.

MESSY
HAIR

GREEN
GLASSES

CAPE

T-SHIRT

LENNY

7

Her signature green glasses were missing. Her hair was longer and curlier than Beatrice remembered. It wasn't regular curly either. It was the kind of curly you get with a curling iron. And a lot of time in front of a mirror with your mother.

But that wasn't the worst part.

Lenny had promised to wear her ninja suit.

The girl staring back at Beatrice was not wearing a ninja suit. She was not, in fact, wearing a single item of black clothing. She wasn't even wearing jeans and a superhero T-shirt like Lenny usually wore.

Nothing about her outfit said "cofounder of a top-secret operation."

Not-quite-Lenny wore a skirt and a pink ruffled sweater that sparkled like a disco ball. She walked right up to Beatrice, pointing at her outfit.

"Wow," said the Lenny-look-alike. "You really wore it."

Maybe it was the real Lenny after all.

"Where's yours?" Beatrice wanted to know. "Did your mom say no?"

"Not exactly," said Lenny, really slow.

A million hopeful possibilities ran through Beatrice's mind.

"Is it in your backpack? Or under that sweater?"

"No." Lenny batted Beatrice's hand away and bit her lip. "To be honest, I forgot all about it."

That seemed impossible.

"But we made plans," said Beatrice.

"That was a long time ago, Beatrice. We were in second grade."

It was only three months ago. Back when Lenny had straight hair and thought wearing a ninja suit was the best idea ever.

"I have an idea," said Beatrice. "What if we scope out our base today, and then we both wear our ninja suits tomorrow?"

"I don't know," said Lenny. "I'm not sure mine fits me anymore."

Beatrice tilted her head to the side. It was true— Lenny did look taller. But maybe it was just the curls.

Lenny leaned in and lowered her voice.

Beatrice stepped closer.

"There's someone I want you to meet," Lenny said. "Just be cool, okay?"

"I'm always cool," said Beatrice.

"Just be normal then?"

Lenny stepped to the side and revealed the tallest third grader Beatrice had ever seen. Lenny waved her forward. "This is Chloe, my new neighbor. She just moved in."

"Hi," said Beatrice, looking up at Chloe.

"Hey," said Chloe, looking down at Beatrice.

"Beatrice is the one I told you about," Lenny added.

Relief rushed through Beatrice. Lenny had forgotten their official plans over the summer, but at least she hadn't forgotten her completely.

Then Lenny said something else.

"She's the one with the sister in fifth grade."

"The sister who runs the foreign-language club?" Chloe asked.

Beatrice blinked her eyes and shook her head. Even suited up in a ninja costume, there are certain things you are never prepared to hear.

"Your sister's club sounds like a great way to meet new friends," said Chloe.

Lenny threw her arm around Chloe. "Will you talk to Kate for us?"

No words came to Beatrice.

She just stood there, thinking.

She wasn't thinking of an answer for Lenny. Instead, she pictured Mrs. Jenkins and her cat, and how today was not supposed to go like this.

Mrs. Tamarack closed the door and clapped her hands. "Find your seats, class!"

Before Beatrice could recover her voice, Lenny walked off in search of her seat. She located her name at a desk near the door. "Look, Chloe—your desk is right next to mine." Chloe dropped her

* ALL HEIGHTS ARE APPROXIMATE,
  BASED SOLELY ON BEATRICE'S IMAGINATION.

shiny purple backpack on the desk adjacent to Lenny's.

Beatrice trailed after them, searching for her spot nearby.

Mrs. Tamarack called her name. "I put you right here, Beatrice," she told her, patting the tabletop at the front of the room. "Where I can keep an eye on you."

The room quieted.

Beatrice felt everyone's eyes as she slid into her seat.

Mrs. Tamarack stood directly in front of her. "Good morning, class," she announced. "Welcome to third grade!"

Beatrice checked the clock.

There were exactly eighty-seven minutes until recess.

She had eighty-seven minutes to fix things with Lenny. Eighty-seven minutes to coordinate a rendezvous point. And eighty-seven minutes to make a plan.

None of that worried Beatrice.

But this did: her desk was right under Mrs. Tamarack's nose. She had exactly eighty-seven minutes to stay out of trouble—or recess was gone, and it was all for nothing.

Operation Upside was doomed.

8
EIGHTY-SEVEN MINUTES

Mrs. Tamarack watched her like a hawk.
With the threat of losing recess looming over
her and Operation Upside
in jeopardy, Beatrice was
on her best behavior.
Nevertheless, the
morning was filled with
one misunderstanding
after another. . . .

Beatrice knew better than to argue.

Instead she kept her chin up and waited for a moment to catch Lenny alone. At midmorning Mrs. Tamarack made an announcement. "Once you finish your All About Me project, turn it in to me, and then you may visit the activity center at the back of the room."

Beatrice seized the opportunity.

She scribbled her name on the back of her poster, then wandered toward the opposite end of the classroom. She paused at Lenny's desk on the way. "Want to do a puzzle?"

"Sure," said Lenny, grabbing another marker. "I'm almost done."

While Lenny added finishing touches to her poster, Beatrice dumped a bag of puzzle pieces on the rug at the back of the room. Her fingers quickly went to work, flipping the cardboard right side up.

Beatrice picked up her favorite piece, cleared a space in the center of the carpet, and dropped it right in the middle. She smiled at the solitary shape—mostly green, surrounded by a sea of possibility.

"Earth to Beatrice," said Lenny, waving a hand in front of her face. She and Chloe plopped down next to her on the floor.

"Which puzzle are you doing?" asked Chloe.

"I'm not sure what it is yet," Beatrice admitted.

Chloe looked around. "Well, where's the box?"

"I left it over there," said Beatrice, pointing at the shelves.

Chloe walked over to the puzzles. "We can just look at the picture on the front."

"I never look at the picture," said Beatrice.

"You don't?"

"She doesn't," said Lenny.

"It ruins the surprise," said Beatrice. "I just start with a piece I like and see where it goes."

"But you didn't even do the edges first," said Chloe. "That's, like, Puzzles 101."

Beatrice shrugged. "If I had to start with the edges, I don't think I'd ever do a puzzle."

While Chloe flipped through puzzle boxes on the rack, Beatrice leaned toward Lenny and whispered, "We don't have a lot of time. We need a plan for recess."

"Oh," said Lenny. "Chloe invited me to play veterinarian with her." She twirled a puzzle piece in her fingers. "I sort of said yes."

"You said yes?"

"Being new isn't easy," Lenny told her. She lifted a shoulder. "And I like her."

"But this is important—we have spying to discuss." Beatrice scooted closer and muffled her voice. "I have a list of possible candidates."

Lenny raised an eyebrow.

"Hey, Lenny, look at this one!" Chloe held up a box with a unicorn on the front. "Isn't it cute?" Chloe tucked the box under her arm.

"Let's do it at our desk. There's more room to spread out the pieces." She walked to her desk without waiting for Lenny to reply.

Lenny mouthed sorry to Beatrice, then hopped up and followed Chloe to their seats. Beatrice blinked at Lenny's back and watched her friend fly away on the wings of the new girl and her sparkly purple unicorn.

9
SOMETHING
UNEXPECTED

Beatrice went back to her seat and tore a sheet of paper from one of her brand-new notebooks. In red ink she wrote Lenny a message. It said:

MEET ME AT THE
WOODEN PLAYGROUND
11:00. COME ALONE.

But it didn't look like that.
It looked like this:

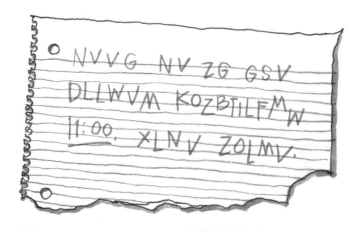

Nothing beat Pig Latin, but occasionally reverse alphabetic code saved the day.

She folded the paper into a square and drew an *L* on the front. She tried to catch Lenny's eye, but the cofounder of Operation Upside was too busy piecing together the edges of the unicorn puzzle and laughing with Chloe.

Beatrice ran through her other options.

She could toss the note—ninja-star-style—in Lenny's direction, but that didn't seem like a good idea. Her aim wasn't great, and it probably wouldn't end well. With Mrs. Tamarack on high alert, a direct delivery seemed like the safest solution.

She just needed an excuse to pass Lenny's desk without drawing attention.

Beatrice opened her pencil box. She grabbed a handful of new pencils and a sharpener. She twisted and turned until the case bulged with shavings.

Her hand shot up in the air, the sharpener still in her grasp.

Mrs. Tamarack sighed. "Yes, Beatrice?"

"May I please empty my pencil sharpener?"

Shavings fluttered down on her desk like volcanic ash.

"Yes, Beatrice," said Mrs. Tamarack, "please do."

With the note cupped in one palm and her sharpener in the other, Beatrice headed toward the trash. Her route put Lenny within range.

Beatrice counted her steps. She would be at Lenny's desk in . . .

Five.

Four.

Three.

On two, Beatrice tripped over a shiny purple backpack.

The sharpener flew from her right hand and opened in midair. The note flew from her left hand and landed in the middle of the floor, directly between Lenny and Chloe.

In desperation, Beatrice dove for the note.

Her whole body strained toward her target.

Her arms lengthened and her fingers grew—but it wasn't enough. The top-secret correspondence rested inches out of reach, just beyond her fingertips.

Mrs. Tamarack jumped up just as the pencil shavings rained down. She was not amused. "Beatrice—that's it!"

"THAT'S THREE."

I TRIPPED.

Beatrice's plans for recess scattered like graphite dust all over the carpet.

But then Lenny did something unexpected.

She did exactly what the old Lenny would have done.

Sliding her leg into the aisle, she covered the exposed note with her shoe and dragged it under her desk, out of view. The expression on her face gave nothing away.

NEW SOCKS
NEW SHOES

OLD LENNY
THING TO DO

Beatrice held her breath.

Lenny wasn't done yet. Smiling at Mrs. Tamarack, she raised her hand.

Mrs. Tamarack sighed again. "Yes, Lenny?"

"I just wanted to say that it looked like an accident to me," she said. "And—to be honest—Beatrice has always been kind of klutzy."

The whole class laughed in agreement.

Mrs. Tamarack narrowed her eyes. She looked between Beatrice and Lenny and the purple backpack on the floor.

A tiny bubble of hope floated up in Beatrice's chest.

"Okay," said Mrs. Tamarack, drawing out the word. "But, Beatrice, be more careful in the future. Go grab the vacuum and clean up this mess before it ruins the carpet."

"I'm still on two then?" said Beatrice.

"You are still on two."

Staring straight ahead, Lenny deposited the note into the pocket of her skirt.

The tiny bubble of hope in Beatrice grew so big it almost hurt.

"So recess is still a go?"

Mrs. Tamarack rubbed her temples. "If you can stay upright for the next five minutes, yes."

"Thank you, thank you," said Beatrice. "You won't be sorry."

10
NOT-AT-ALL
SECRETIVE

Six minutes later, after putting away the vacuum, Beatrice squinted in the sunlight and surveyed the playground. The old wooden structure at the back of the lot was the perfect meeting spot. Tall oak trees created a natural camouflage. Plus, it was usually deserted. When the school installed a new playscape closer to the sandbox the year before, everyone forgot about the old, splintery one in the back.

Everyone except Lenny and Beatrice.

It was more than a perfect meeting spot—it was the perfect location for their secret base.

Getting there without being seen was the tricky part. A soccer tournament and a game of kickball made the ground too exposed. And tree trunks offered minimal protection.

Up was the only option.

Beatrice lifted herself into the branches of the nearest tree.

The view was amazing.

With a panorama of the playground, she plotted her course. Ninja-nimble, feline-flexible, and doggedly determined, Beatrice used all her best moves.

TREETOP
TRAPEZE

WALK
THE
PLANK

THE
STiCKY
GECKO

As Beatrice neared her destination, she heard Lenny's voice down below.

"This is it!" Lenny announced. "Isn't it perfect?"

Lenny's voice was loud and not-at-all secretive.

"I forgot all about this place!" said another voice. It was familiar, but Beatrice couldn't place it. Then a third voice joined in.

"It's a little rickety, but it should work. . . ."

Beatrice recognized Chloe's voice immediately.

She dropped through the branches to get a better view. Lenny stood in front of the wooden doorway. Chloe and three other girls circled around her.

What was Lenny thinking?

She had led everyone straight to their rendezvous point!

As the girls wandered inside to explore, Beatrice got Lenny's attention. "Psst!" she said. "Up here."

Lenny blinked into the branches. "Beatrice? What are you doing up there?"

"I was just asking the same question. What are YOU doing?"

"I'm playing veterinarian," said Lenny. "I told you that."

Beatrice lowered her voice. "Didn't you read my note?"

Lenny leaned up on tiptoe, her eyes wide. "I couldn't figure it out," she said, grimacing. "I really tried."

It wasn't the first time they had run into this problem.

"It was reverse alphabetic code," said Beatrice. "*A* equals *Z*."

"You know I'm not very good at codes. I need a key."

"Plus you don't have your glasses on," Beatrice pointed out. Then she had to ask— "Why don't you have your glasses on?"

"Beatrice, what if this is my moment, and I need to take it?" Lenny wasn't making any sense. "Your moment for what?" asked Beatrice.

"For things to be different," said Lenny.

Beatrice tilted her head. "You want to be a veterinarian?"

"No," said Lenny, "but don't you ever wish you were different?"

Beatrice shook her head and told the truth. "Not really."

"Well," said Lenny, pushing up glasses that weren't there, "not everyone can be like you."

"I know that," said Beatrice.

Lenny didn't look convinced. She was about to say more, but Chloe called her name. "Lenny—where'd you go?" She walked over to Lenny under the tree. "What's up?"

Lenny pointed at Beatrice through the leaves.

Chloe waved. "Oh, hey, Beatrice." She craned her neck, looking confused. "What are you doing up there?"

Beatrice was trying to salvage a top-secret mission with her best friend. But she couldn't tell Chloe that.

Instead Beatrice closed her eyes and made a quick decision—the kind cofounders of secret operations specialize in.

11

BEATRICE IS A BAT

Keeping her legs wrapped tight around the branch, Beatrice swung into position.

"I'm playing veterinarian with you," she told Chloe. "I'll be the monkey."

Chloe shook her head. "Sorry—you can't be a monkey."

"Why not? Are you the monkey?"

"No," said Chloe. "There are no monkeys. I'm the veterinarian."

"Can I be a snake then?"

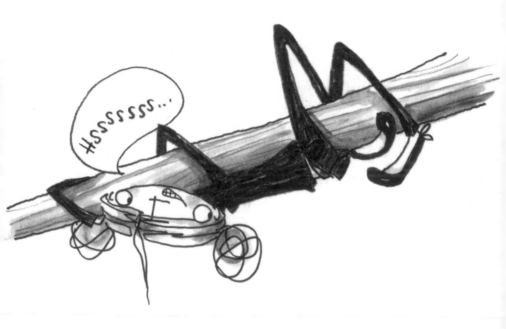

"Ew," said Chloe, "definitely no reptiles."

"What about a sloth?" Beatrice suggested. "They're cute."

"Can't you just be something normal?" Lenny whispered up at her.

"How about a bat? If you really think about it, bats are probably more common than cats."

The other three girls—Grace, Parvati, and Eva—came out to find them.

"I'm a poodle," said Grace.

"I'm a puppy," said Parvati.

"I'll be a cat," Eva volunteered.

"Perfect," said Chloe. She pointed into the tree. "Beatrice is a bat."

Lenny glared up at Beatrice.

Beatrice stared down at Lenny.

Their eyes said all the things they couldn't say out loud.

"Come on, guys," said Chloe. She waved her arm and ducked through the doorway.

Lenny shrugged up at Beatrice, then followed Chloe inside—followed by Grace the Poodle, Parvati the Puppy, and Eva the Cat. One by one, they disappeared—first the two vets, then the three pets.

Beatrice the Bat stayed outside alone, pondering her next move.

Laughter echoed out of the new veterinary clinic. Beatrice didn't know what was so funny, but Lenny laughed the loudest. After a whole summer of preparation, and eighty-seven minutes of third-grade desperation, everything was falling apart.

Luckily, Beatrice knew what she had to do.

EEEK!

Lenny's laughter meant one thing: it was time for an injured wing.

Rocking back and forth, Beatrice gained momentum. On the count of two, she flipped her legs, stretched out her arms, and flew.

"Eeeek!" she screeched in her best bat voice.

She planned to land in a graceful crumple. She planned to clutch her wing and whimper. When they all came out to investigate, she planned to impress them with her pretend-bat skills.

But—like the rest of her day, things didn't go exactly as planned.

The ground arrived sooner than she expected and smacked her in the face.

"Owww!" she screamed, sounding more like a human than a bat.

Lenny rushed out of the clinic. "What was that?"

"It was me," Beatrice mumbled, sprawled on the ground.

"Beatrice!" Lenny screamed.

Chloe rushed out behind her, followed by the trio of pets.

"Eeeek!" screeched Chloe, sounding more like a bat than a vet.

Kids came running from all corners of the playground. It didn't take much to draw a crowd at recess—

Maybe it was Beatrice's bat scream.

Maybe it was her real one.

Maybe it was Lenny's scream.

Or maybe it was the way Chloe hadn't stopped screaming.

Lenny knelt next to Beatrice. Her eyebrows pinched together. "Beatrice, you're bleeding!" she yelled. Her eyebrows didn't pinch together like she was worried—they pinched together like she was mad.

Beatrice touched her face. It was sticky with blood.

Chloe turned pale. "I think I'm going to faint."

Beatrice jumped to her feet, covering her face with her sleeve. "I'm okay!" she announced. "It's only a bloody nose. I was just coming inside to play."

"Ew," said Eva the Cat. "You should probably go see Ms. Cindy instead."

"Uh-huh," the poodle agreed. "You need a nurse."

The puppy nodded her head. "Yeah—before that gets worse."

Chloe groaned and slumped to the ground.

"I planned to see the veterinarian," Beatrice told them, gesturing toward Chloe. "But it doesn't look like that's going to work out."

Lenny frowned at her, fanning Chloe's face.

"Fine," Beatrice announced. "I'll be right back." Raising her chin, she spun around.

The whole crowd took a giant step backward, letting her through.

Only one person didn't back up with the rest— she stepped forward instead.

"What in the world, Beatrice?!" Kate fumed. "I don't understand you. It's the first day of school, and you're already a disaster!"

Beatrice faced her sister as the wall of spectators listened in. All the day's frustration flooded her eyes as blood dripped down her chin.

"Please don't tell Mom." She wiped her nose with her sleeve. "It's really not that bad."

Kate cringed. "One look at your face, and I won't have to say a thing." She looked around. "How'd it happen, anyway?"

Her gaze bounced between Beatrice and Lenny and Chloe on the ground.

Beatrice shrugged and looked away. Everyone was listening, and there was too much to say.

"Well—you better go to the office," Kate told her. "You can't go back to class like that."

Lenny was crouched next to Chloe, reminding her to relax and take deep breaths. Grace, Parvati, and Eva stood nearby, along with the rest of the crowd, waiting to see what Beatrice would do.

Beatrice held up her hands. "Okay!" she huffed, shouldering past Kate. "I was already going anyway."

She pulled the collar of her turtleneck over her face and headed inside. Every step closer to the school put Lenny further away.

12

STILL NOT A PROMISE

The nurse's office hadn't changed over the summer. It was still a mishmash of mismatched furniture and random supplies. The same scuffs marked the walls.

"Is my favorite upside down thinker under there somewhere?"

When Beatrice heard the familiar voice, her whole body relaxed. She tugged the turtleneck away from her face and smiled wryly at Ms. Cindy, the school nurse. "The one and only," she said and took a bow.

The bow turned out to be a mistake.

"Oh dear," said Ms. Cindy. She grabbed a roll of paper towels from her desk and passed Beatrice a generous handful. "Maybe you better lie down. Got yourself good, didn't you?"

"We were playing veterinarian. I was a bat."

"Of course you were," said Ms. Cindy. "I wondered how soon I'd see you this year." Beatrice blotted her face. "First day," Ms. Cindy mused. "That has to be a record—even for you."

"That's me," said Beatrice. "Winner of weird prizes."

"The girl who always surprises," Ms. Cindy fired back.

Beatrice laughed.

"Oh dear," said Ms. Cindy, handing her another wad. "I know I'm funny, but try not to laugh."

"When it stops bleeding, can I go back out there?"

"To the playground?" asked Ms. Cindy. "I don't think so. The real question is if you'll be back in class today."

Beatrice set down the paper towels. "But I'm totally fine."

"Said the girl with blood dripping down her face."

"It's only a bloody nose."

"Health-code policy, I'm afraid. Your outfit needs to go in here." Ms. Cindy held up a doubled plastic bag. "Don't worry, though, I'm going to call your parents to bring you a change of clothes. Anything I can get you from the teachers' lounge? Ice pack? Maybe an ice cream?"

Beatrice shook her head. "No, thanks." She just wanted to get back outside.

"Well, let me know if you change your mind." The nurse handed her the whole roll of towels as she headed out the door. "Here's this—just in case. Why don't you lean your head back and relax while I'm gone?"

Ms. Cindy popped back in a few minutes later. "When I said to lean your head back, I didn't mean *that* far back."

Beatrice sat up. "What'd they say?"

"No answer, but I left them each a message."

"I think they both have meetings today. Did you try our babysitter?" Then Beatrice remembered—it was Tuesday, and Henry had baby-enrichment classes all day. She looked down at her ninja suit. "Are you sure I can't go back in this? You can't even see the blood."

"Sorry, kid," the nurse said. "Tough girl or not, those are the rules."

"I don't care about rules." Beatrice crumbled. "I have to go back!"

Ms. Cindy passed her a tissue. "That one's for your eyes," she told her. "We keep a stash of lost-and-found clothes in that bin behind you, for emergencies. All freshly laundered. You're welcome to dig around and see what you can find while you wait.

"And if you get bored, Mr. Hannah has a bunch of socks in that bag, along with some random art supplies. Sometimes kids make puppets when they talk to him." Mr. Hannah was the school counselor. Beatrice had talked to him on several occasions. He was always very serious. He had never mentioned puppets.

Beatrice wiped her eyes. "Any spare ninja suits around here?"

"I'm afraid we're fresh out," said Ms. Cindy, "but Mrs. Tamarack dropped off your backpack and your lunch. It's right here if you get hungry." She set Beatrice's belongings on a chair by the door. "I'm sure your parents will call back soon. I've got some stuff to take care of. You'll be fine here while I get to it?"

Beatrice nodded.

Her nose throbbed. Her head hurt.

And Lenny didn't want to be a ninja anymore.

Even worse, Lenny didn't want to be Lenny anymore.

Beatrice lifted her thumb. "I'll be fine," she told Ms. Cindy.

STILL NOT A PROMISE

13

WE HAVE A WINNER

The first half hour
Beatrice did nothing
but think.

And think.

And think some more.

She should've been pondering contenders for Operation Upside, or other potential locations for their secret base, but all she could think about was Lenny.

Hoping it would make her feel better, Beatrice broke into her lunch. She scattered the contents on one of the room's many chairs and arranged them in the order she always ate them, from first to last.

Glancing at the clock, her stomach dropped. Lenny and Chloe were probably together in the cafeteria right now, eating lunch in its proper order.

Suddenly she wasn't hungry anymore.

Not even for dessert.

She bagged everything up and zipped it out of sight.

She needed to get out of here.

She studied the scuffed-up door. First-aid posters decorated every inch, but none of them helped with her current emergency. On the other side, Ms. Cindy murmured and moved around, but she didn't come back in. Beatrice counted each time the shadow of her feet passed the crack under the door.

While she waited for Ms. Cindy's return, Beatrice counted other things. Ceiling tiles. Used paper towels. Spiderwebs. The socks in Mr. Hannah's supply bag.

There were seventeen socks and zero matches.

Beatrice slipped a favorite onto each hand. Then she checked her nose.

It was still bleeding.

"Look at you," Beatrice said to her left hand, "you're a mess."

"You look a little rough yourself."

"It's been a rough day," Beatrice admitted.

"Good thing it's not over yet," said her other hand.

"Wow," said Beatrice. "You're right. It isn't over." There was still time to turn things around.

Gathering a fresh wad of paper towels, she covered her nose and secured the paper towel in place with her turtleneck.

Then, squaring her shoulders, Beatrice stood tall.

She was the cofounder of a secret operation. She couldn't give up. Not on Operation Upside. And never on Lenny.

If the mission ever mattered, it mattered now.

Beatrice marched to the emergency clothes bin, determined to find something to wear, determined to get back to Lenny. The blue lid popped off with a snap.

TOO FLORAL

"It's time to take matters into my own hands," she said.

TOO SCARY

TOO FESTIVE

A tangle of cast-off clothing filled the container. Beatrice took a deep breath and dug in.

She considered each item, one by one.

too FAIRY

Then she tossed them
aside, two by two . . .

and too by too.

too FUZZY

too
SLOUCHY

TOO
STRIPEY

TOO
GROUCHY

NOPE.

When she reached
the bottom of the
bin, she collapsed on
her knees. "No wonder
no one wanted these."

Her right hand spoke up.

MAYBE YOU NEED TO LOOK AT it ANOTHER WAY. . .

"Like what?"

"Like, what if any minute now, your mother shows up with that dress?"

Beatrice sat up. Anything was better than that dress. She closed her eyes and reached into the pile again. Her hands pulled out a pair of plaid pants and a cable-knit sweater. The sweater was too scratchy. The pants were too patchy.

THAT DRESS

But Beatrice didn't care anymore.

She held the outfit high in triumph.

"We have a winner, folks!"

The tide was turning. Even her nose cooperated and finally stopped bleeding.

Beatrice tossed the used paper towel into the trash. The evidence of her injury disappeared into the bin, nothing but net. With her nose dry and her hope renewed, Beatrice wasted no time changing.

She stuffed her contaminated ninja suit inside the plastic bag from Ms. Cindy, then buried the bag in her backpack. She peeled off the puppets and packed them inside, too. "I'll talk to you guys later," she told them before she zipped them up. She repacked the lost-and-found bin and pushed it back where she'd found it.

Just like that, Operation Upside was back in business. Beatrice didn't have a plan yet—but at least she was on her way back to Lenny.

14

A PRETTY GREAT DISGUISE

Beatrice stuck her head out the door.

"Ms. Cindy?" she called. "I'm ready to go back to class."

Ms. Cindy didn't answer.

Beatrice tried again. "Hello?"

No one answered.

She tiptoed into the main office and looked around. The phones were ringing. Both desks were empty, and no one was in sight.

Something on the counter caught her eye.

Sitting there, in all their bright green glory, were Lenny's glasses. A piece of yellow scrap paper was tucked beneath them.

It said: FOR ELEANOR SANTOS.

The phones stopped ringing. All sound was sucked out of the air. The whole office disappeared. All that existed was a pair of glasses and three special words.

In that moment, with Lenny's official name spelled out in front of her, the first task of Operation Upside became clear. The day started rough, but it would end on an UPSIDE. She knew exactly how to make it happen.

If she did anything today, she would get this right.

The details of the plan fell into place as she perfected her costume. One brief stop into forbidden territory without getting caught, and the rest would be easy.

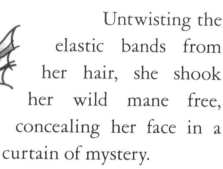

Untwisting the elastic bands from her hair, she shook her wild mane free, concealing her face in a curtain of mystery.

As the final touch, Beatrice picked up Lenny's green frames and put them on.

It wasn't a ninja suit—and she could barely see—but it was a pretty great disguise.

Before she left, she turned over the yellow paper and left a message for Ms. Cindy.

She hoped it was enough to cover her tracks.

15
THE END OF THE LINE

Beatrice didn't have a hall pass, but she marched down the main corridor of William Charles Elementary like she belonged there. Chin up, eyes straight ahead, her confident stride carried her past one teacher, three fifth graders, and a long line of kindergartners. No one gave her a second look.

She didn't slow down until she reached the end of the line.

THE END OF THE LINE →

TEACHERS' LOUNGE

Everything she needed was on the other side. Beatrice gathered her courage, counted to three, and turned the knob. She stepped over the threshold into the teachers' lounge, like she did it all the time.

The room was smaller than she expected.

A wooden conference table filled up most of the floor. A kitchenette covered one wall. Storage cabinets lined another.

After surveying the space, Beatrice grabbed the metal handle on a cabinet marked PAPER. She closed her eyes and hoped for the best. "Be open, be open," she whispered. After a jiggle and wiggle, and a little force, the latch gave way.

A rainbow of paper packed the shelves. Beatrice searched the stacks, leafing for something very specific. Something shimmery. On the bottom shelf, in a pile of scraps and leftovers, Beatrice found exactly what she came for.

Next she scavenged for a pen. The third cabinet down housed a paradise of writing implements. Sliding Lenny's glasses into her hair, she tapped her lip and assessed her options. She smiled when she saw a box marked GOLD.

Nothing was more official than glittering gold lettering.

Beatrice pulled out a chair and arranged her supplies on the table. For a minute she just sat there, taking it all in, envisioning the document she needed to create.

When she was ready, she uncapped a pen and practiced her letters on a piece of scrap paper. She scribbled. She looped. She twirled. With each experiment, her confidence grew.

Her handwriting looked good in gold.

She smoothed the special paper in front of her. Closing her eyes, she breathed in deep and pressed her pen to the real thing. The shiny ink glided across the smooth surface.

She crafted each letter with precision. After inscribing all the words, she puffed her cheeks and blew them dry with a gentle breeze. She tested the ink with her fingertips, then slid the paper into a folder for protection. With a thick red marker, she marked it CONFIDENTIAL.

The capital letters made her smile.

Operation Upside was happening, and it was happening today.

She tucked the folder into her backpack and tossed it over her shoulder. With her hand on the doorknob, and her heart pounding in anticipation, Beatrice flicked off the light. Her stomach let out a rumble of protest.

Beatrice paused as a new idea sparked to life in her mind.

It was too perfect to pass up.

Flicking the light back on, Beatrice backtracked to the kitchenette and yanked open the freezer. She hopped onto the counter to get a better look.

Deep in the back, Beatrice hit the jackpot.

Behind a stack of microwave lasagnas was an unopened box of ice-cream cones.

But before she claimed her prize, there was something she needed to do. Beatrice jumped down, grabbed a piece of paper, and made Ms. Cindy an IOU.

Smiling, Beatrice unzipped her bag and deposited three pre-packaged cones inside.

Things were looking up. And this was the cherry on top.

She dropped Lenny's green glasses back into place. Everything was blurry again, but Beatrice was focused. She took a deep breath, flipped the light switch, and headed into the hall.

It was time to find her friend.

HI

I CHANGed my mind aBout the ICE cream.

I o u!
—B.Z.

16

INTO THE TREES

Classroom 3B was dark and empty when Beatrice slipped inside. The screaming sounds of recess seeped through the windows. Beatrice lifted up the blinds, and Lenny's glasses, to get a better view.

Second recess was in full swing. If she hurried, she could still get to Lenny with enough time to properly kick off Operation Upside.

Beatrice found the door and pushed her way outside into the light.

A kickball flew past her head.

A rush of teammates trampled in front of her, shouting, "Get it! Get it!"

Beatrice weaved through the chaos to the tree

THE SCAREDY SQUIRREL

line. She scrambled up the first trunk and charted her path to the back of the playground. Just as she was about to make her first move, a crisp breeze swept through the trees, rustling the leaves and sending a chill down her spine.

Beatrice froze. She held her breath and gripped the trunk, hoping it was nothing.

A branch snapped beneath her.

Then came the voice.

"Where do you think you're going in that getup?"

It was not nothing.

It was Evelyn Tamarack.

← — SOMETHING

Her teacher scowled up at her, whistle in her mouth, at the ready.

↖ SMALL BUT FRIGHTENING

Beatrice stared down at Mrs. Tamarack's blurry face.

She needed to stay calm.

She needed to stick to the truth.

Ninjas did this kind of thing all the time.

"I'm on my way to see Lenny," she stated. "It's important."

Mrs. Tamarack nodded. She circled the tree, her whistle still between her lips. "I have a message for you—from Ms. Cindy." Reaching into her pocket, she extracted a slip of paper and snapped it open. The note flapped in the breeze.

Beatrice closed her eyes and braced herself for the impending doom.

She should have waited in the office.

She should have waited for Ms. Cindy's permission.

Mrs. Tamarack cleared her throat. "Ms. Cindy wanted you to know that she talked to your mother," she said. "Apparently she was on her way to school with another outfit, but Ms. Cindy let her know that you already found a change of clothes."

"Oh." Beatrice exhaled into the tree trunk. "Okay."

"Ms. Cindy also said to thank you for delivering Eleanor's glasses." Mrs. Tamarack paused over her words, like it was difficult to say them. "She said you were very helpful."

Beatrice lifted her head and nodded at Mrs. Tamarack. "Please tell Ms. Cindy I was happy to accept the mission."

Mrs. Tamarack narrowed her eyes. Her whistle shrilled a little.

Beatrice steadied herself on the branch.

"You'll get to tell her yourself if you're not more careful up there," Mrs. Tamarack scolded. "Is something wrong with the ground?"

Beatrice peered down at her teacher. Her eyes shifted across the field to the wooden playground tucked in the back. From her perch, Beatrice could see exactly where she needed to go. Everything seemed possible. She grasped the trunk tighter and shrugged. "I just like the trees."

Mrs. Tamarack's whistle wiggled between her lips. Her hands clenched on her hips.

"I'd better go," Beatrice said quickly. She pointed at the glasses on her face. "Lenny needs these."

Mrs. Tamarack pinched the bridge of her nose. "Make it quick, Miss Zinker. Recess is almost over."

17

IT'S A SIGN

When Beatrice reached the play structure, something was different. A paper sign hung above the open doorway. Masking tape held it in place. Thick black letters spelled out the word VET.

It was official. Chloe's clinic had staked its claim to the best spot on the playground.

Staring at the sign, the loss bothered Beatrice less than it did earlier. If things didn't work out, Operation Upside would find another headquarters.

Some losses were worse than others.

A secret base was replaceable. Lenny Santos was not.

Dropping onto the roof, Beatrice shrugged her backpack off her shoulders and prepared to make her entrance. She began with Lenny's glasses. The world crystallized as she lifted the frames from her face and slipped them into her back pocket to keep them safe.

The hat came next. She stuffed it into the bottom of her bag, next to the folder marked CONFIDENTIAL. Flipping her head upside down, Beatrice parted the tangle of hair. Her fingers spun each handful into shape and secured both sides with elastic.

She hooked her backpack on a nearby branch, setting it aside for later.

Following the clamor of animal noises to the back of the building, she crawled to the edge of the roof and peeked below. Inside were plenty of pretend pets, and plenty of pretend pet owners, but Lenny was nowhere in sight.

Unfazed, Beatrice crept to the front and checked the window by the door.

Bingo.

Lenny and Chloe were huddled together, debating who would diagnose a sick hamster and who would help a husky with a broken leg.

Beatrice rapped on the wall. "Knock, knock."

Chloe looked up. Lenny turned around. When they saw her, Chloe folded her arms and Lenny frowned.

"Please tell me you are not a bat," said Chloe.

Beatrice shook her head. "I'm done with that. But I do have a new idea—if you're ready?"

Lenny and Chloe looked less than ready.

Beatrice filled her lungs and proceeded anyway. "So . . . what if this place looks like an ordinary vet clinic to the average eye, but—in reality—it's the headquarters of a top-secret organization?"

"Beatrice . . ." Lenny groaned.

"What?"

Chloe sighed. "There are two things you should know." She held up her index finger. "First of all, this is no ordinary facility. We are world renowned." Another finger joined the first. "Second—we do not participate in illegal activities."

"What if it's legal—good, even?" Beatrice lowered her voice. "Just a secret?"

"We're just a nice, normal clinic, Beatrice," said Lenny.

"Exactly," said Chloe. "I don't like secrets."

With that, she spun on her heel and walked away. She headed out of the room—toward the hamster, the husky, and all the other pets who needed her attention. Beatrice waited until Chloe stepped out of earshot, then she motioned Lenny over to the window.

Lenny took two steps forward, her whole face a frown.

"Don't worry," said Beatrice. "I have a back-up plan." She rubbed her hands together with anticipation. "Want to hear it?"

"I don't know, Beatrice." Lenny kicked the dirt with her toe. Dust billowed in a cloud around her. "I'm still a little mad."

Sunlight snuck through the wood slats of the structure, covering Lenny in stripes. Her sparkly sweater flashed at Beatrice, each flicker an accusation.

"I'm sorry," Beatrice told Lenny, shielding her eyes. Her voice got quiet. "I didn't mean to ruin your moment."

"It's okay," said Lenny. Her eyes floated to Chloe in the distance. "You didn't. Not really."

"So do you want to hear my idea?"

"Fine," Lenny sighed. She didn't look excited, but she wasn't frowning anymore.

Beatrice nodded toward Chloe. "What if we let Chloe be Chloe—a normal medical professional, just like she said?" Beatrice leaned forward, her eyes glowing. "But what if you—Lenny Santos—are undercover? You could be a secret agent *disguised* as a veterinarian. You could be the secret eyes of our operation."

Lenny glanced back at Chloe and fought a smile.

"You'll need a code name. And we need an emergency signal and a password as soon as possible. You should also brush up on your Pig Latin and your decoding skills, of course."

Lenny laughed. "I didn't say yes yet, you know."

"I know." Beatrice reached into her pocket.

"But, either way—you'll need these."

Stretching her arm, Beatrice held out her hand. Her fingers unfolded like a flower. Lenny's bright green glasses rested in her palm.

"Hey!" Lenny grabbed her specs. "Where did you get these?"

"They turned up in my travels."

Lenny slid her glasses over her ears.

"Better?" Beatrice asked. She reached over and pulled the veterinary sign off the doorway. "Can you read this?"

She flipped it around. "What about now?"

Behind her glasses, Lenny's eyes grew.
Her mouth fell open.

"It says my name." She grabbed the paper from
Beatrice's fingers. "How'd you do that?"

"I don't know." Beatrice studied the letters. "I
think it's a sign."

"Well, duh," said Lenny.

"No, I think it's trying to tell us something."

"Like what?"

"Maybe that it's okay to be more than one thing?"

"Huh," said Lenny, flipping the paper back and forth, contemplating the changing words.

"So what say you, Lenny Santos?"

The corner of Lenny's mouth turned up. "I say maybe."

"Maybe's good," said Beatrice.

Maybe was very good.

"I'll be in contact," Beatrice told her. "Expect me when you least expect me." She gave Lenny a thumbs-up. "And that's a promise."

Beatrice taped Chloe's sign back in place above the door and disappeared into the trees.

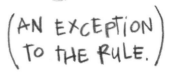

(AN EXCEPTION TO THE RULE.)

18

THAT SPECIAL PIECE
OF THE PUZZLE

Mrs. Tamarack's whistle rang across the playground.

It was the warning call.

Recess was winding down. Beatrice had five minutes to complete her task.

Whether Lenny was officially in or officially out, Beatrice was determined to deliver the document in her backpack. Even after the day she'd had, Beatrice believed in the magic of Operation Upside.

Executing the entire plan would take weeks, maybe months. If they spied on everyone, it might last all year. But, today, Beatrice would make the first move.

Balanced high in the bough of her favorite tree, she reached into her backpack and grabbed the confidential folder. She lifted the cover and studied the crisp piece of paper inside.

It shimmered in the sunlight like Lenny's new sweater.

The rightness of it filled her chest. Like that special piece of a puzzle, it was a perfect way to begin.

Far below, Lenny stood outside the wooden doorway of Chloe's clinic, smiling. With her hands in her back pockets, she studied the VET sign.

Her hair was still curly. Her sweater was still sparkly.

But Lenny looked like Lenny again.

Maneuvering through the branches, Beatrice dropped down next to her friend.

"One more thing, Lenny."

Lenny spun around with her hand on her chest. "Beatrice!" she screamed. "Are you crazy?"

"I warned you to expect me when you least expect me."

Lenny looked into the leaves above her head. "But you just left."

"Exactly," said Beatrice.

Lenny grinned. "I guess you win, then."

"Actually you win," Beatrice said. "That's why I'm here." She pulled the folder from behind her back and presented the award to Lenny. "Today I realized the first UPSIDE had to go to you."

Lenny looked up at Beatrice, then down at the paper in her hands. She adjusted her glasses as her eyes moved over the words, tracing and retracing the gold letters.

"I don't know what to say."

Beatrice knew exactly how Lenny felt.

Three months ago, standing in the gym with her own award, she felt the exact same way.

"I know we planned to pick people together—and after this we will—but if anyone deserves to know how great they are, it's you."

Beatrice reached behind her.

"Hold on," she said. "There's one more part." She dug the ice cream out of her backpack. "We need to do this right."

She ripped the plastic wrap with her teeth and aimed the cone at Lenny.

"Lenny Santos, how does it feel to be an award winner?"

"Kind of amazing."
Lenny grabbed the mic
and took a giant melty bite.
"Really, really great." She
couldn't stop smiling.

Beatrice tore the wrapper
on the other microphone.
"What do you think of the
name Operation Upside?" she
asked Lenny.

Lenny took another bite,
considering. "I think it's perfect," she decided. "But
if you pick the name—I get to pick the password.
And maybe sometimes you could be a cat?"

Beatrice laughed and bonked her cone on Lenny's. "Deal," she said.

With a mouthful of ice cream, Lenny leaned against the tree and looked around. "So who gets the next one?"

"Well, we still need to do a lot of reconnaissance, but I think the next play should be up to you."

Lenny glanced back into the veterinary clinic where Chloe was giving orders. She bit her lip, hesitating. "What about an edge piece?"

Beatrice followed Lenny's eyes. "Chloe?" Beatrice turned the idea over in her mind and smiled. "I like it."

Chloe had single-handedly started a world renowned veterinary clinic on her first day at a new school. It was hard not to like that, at least a little bit.

"You do?" Lenny said.

"I had a lot of time to think today. Just because I'm upside down doesn't mean everyone has to be. Isn't that the whole point?"

Lenny borrowed Beatrice's word. "Wow," she said.

"She can't know it was us, so we still have a lot of planning to do." Beatrice reached into her backpack and pulled out the third cone. "But for now, do you think she'd want some ice cream?"

Lenny lifted her eyebrows. "You brought her one?"

"Everyone likes ice cream, right?" Beatrice shrugged her shoulders. "And someone told me it's not easy to be the new girl."

"You heard it here first," Lenny announced into her cone.

Mrs. Tamarack's final whistle echoed through the trees.

Beatrice looked into the branches above her head. "Think Chloe will go back to class my way?"

Lenny laughed. "Not a chance in the world."

"I didn't think so." Beatrice flipped to the ground. "Okay," she said, "we'll do it her way."

Lenny leaned into the clinic. "Hey, Chloe—want to walk back with us?"

Chloe appeared in the doorway.

Beatrice held up the cones. "I brought ice cream."

"I see that." Chloe looked confused. "Where'd it come from?"

Lenny turned to Beatrice and pointed at their cones. "Yeah—where did you get these?"

Beatrice smiled mysteriously, handing Chloe her own cone. "Sorry," she said. "Some secrets are just meant to be enjoyed."

With the treetops shading their way, they headed back to class, enjoying every bite.

19
THE LONG WAY HOME

Beatrice evaded her sister after school. She wasn't ready for another lecture, so she lingered at the back of the bus until Kate and her friends hopped out. Then she crossed the street and took the scenic route.

The long way home went right by Mrs. Jenkins's house. As usual, her neighbor was sitting on her front steps, reading to her cat. As usual, Scrappy was drinking tea and listening attentively.

"Hi, Mrs. Jenkins." Beatrice waved, walking over.

"Hello, dear." Mrs. Jenkins patted the spot next to her. "Tell me about your day," she invited. "You look like you have a story—and you know how I love stories."

Beatrice dropped her backpack and plopped down with a sigh. "It was a weird day." She paused, deciding how to talk about her day without revealing top-secret information. Finally she started with, "Remember Lenny?"

"Of course I remember Lenny! I want to steal those green glasses of hers."

"Me too," said Beatrice, glad she got to try them out. "Lenny was gone all summer, so I was really excited to see her. But everything was different.

"She forgot to wear her ninja suit and only wanted to play veterinarian with this new girl, Chloe.

Then I was a bat and got a bloody nose and spent half the day in the office." Beatrice took a deep breath and scooped Scrappy into her lap. "But it's okay now—we worked it out." She buried her face in Scrappy's soft fur. "I should have known we would."

"Life's like that." Mrs. Jenkins nodded her head knowingly. "It's always shifting and changing. That's why most friendships last only for a season. But occasionally you find a really special one—and you grow with each other, instead of apart."

Beatrice hoped her friendship with Lenny was the unusual kind.

Mrs. Jenkins lifted a pitcher of golden liquid. "Want some tea?"

The brew glowed in the sunlight. Tiny ice cubes made music against the glass.

"Yes, please," said Beatrice.

Mrs. Jenkins filled a tall glass from the bright green tray at her side.

"Here you are," she said.

Beatrice lifted the glass to her lips. The tea tasted exactly like it looked—like Mrs. Jenkins had captured all the bittersweet beauty of the day just so she could drink it up.

Down the block, Kate was standing at their door, saying good-bye to her friends. Everywhere she went, Kate had a lot of friends.

Beatrice jiggled her ice cubes and stole a glance at Mrs. Jenkins. "Do you have a sister?"

"Oh do I!" Mrs. Jenkins laughed and slapped her leg. "Drove her crazy for eighteen years—then she moved clear across the country. You can't pick your family, can you?"

Beatrice shook her head. You couldn't.

And they couldn't pick you, either.

Mrs. Jenkins nudged her elbow. "But you know what's funny?"

Beatrice shrugged. "Not really." Nothing seemed particularly funny when Kate was probably in the house complaining about her right that second.

"Now my sister calls me every day. We couldn't be more different, but deep down, there's no one more the same. I wish we'd realized that when we were younger."

Beatrice tipped back the last of her tea, trying to picture ways she and Kate were anything alike.

The Zinkers' babysitter peeked her head out the front door, frowning. Her eyes searched up and down the street, then squinted up into the trees. Beatrice set down her glass and handed the cat to Mrs. Jenkins. "I better go. Daphne gets worried when I don't come right home."

Mrs. Jenkins patted her hand. "I understand, dear. They're lucky to have you. Come back tomorrow. The tea will be here, and so will we."

Beatrice took the front steps two at time. "I'm here, Daphne!" she announced as she bounded through the door. She made a beeline for the laundry room and tossed her backpack onto the floor.

In the kitchen, Kate was telling Henry and Daphne all about her first day of school.

Beatrice lifted the lid on the washer and dumped her ninja suit inside. Operation Upside had survived its first day, but for the cofounder of a top-secret organization, the work was never done. After a drizzle of detergent and the push of a button, the machine started to hum. Kate's voice faded as the room filled with the sound of water and bubbles and a fresh start tomorrow.

Beatrice slung her backpack over her shoulder and ventured down the hall. She stopped in the kitchen doorway.

"Want a snack?" Daphne held up a plate of vegetables. "We're practicing our French." Henry and Daphne sat on one side of the kitchen table, nibbling baby-sized veggies. Kate sat across from them, holding up flash cards.

Kate's eyes flicked up and met hers, then drifted to her nose. Despite Mrs. Jenkins's story, Beatrice couldn't imagine an older version of Kate calling her every day.

Beatrice shook her head at Daphne.

"No, thanks," she told her. "I have some stuff I need to do." Pointing behind her as she backed up the steps, she said, "I'll be in my room."

20

A PIECE OF CAKE

Beatrice had just started to relax when Kate's footsteps thudded up the stairs. She peeked her head around the corner and asked, "Are you okay?"

Daphne must have sent Kate up to check on her.

"*Ep-yay*," said Beatrice. "Just practicing my Pig Latin."

Kate leaned against the wall. "Mom just called," she said. "They're almost home with dinner." She chewed her thumbnail, staring at Beatrice. "Just so you know, I didn't say anything about recess—but she already knew."

"Ms. Cindy called her," Beatrice confessed. "Did she sound mad?"

"Actually, no. If anything, she seemed worried about you."

Beatrice let out a sigh of relief. Kate tilted her head, studying Beatrice's face. "It looks a lot better than it did earlier," she said.

Beatrice's cheeks felt hot. It was an almost-apology. And, from Kate, it was a lot.

"Thanks," Beatrice told her.

"So who was that girl with Lenny?"

"That's Chloe—Lenny's new neighbor. She's a veterinarian."

"You mean a vegetarian?"

"No," said Beatrice. "Well, maybe—she might be. She takes her animals very seriously."

Thinking about Chloe reminded Beatrice of the request Lenny had made first thing that morning. "Hey, Kate?" Beatrice said. She made herself ask the question before she changed her mind. "I have a question."

"Uh-oh," said Kate, standing up straighter.

"Do you have room in your foreign-language club for Lenny and Chloe?" Beatrice asked. "They think it's a good way to meet new friends."

"Sure," Kate said easily. "There's always room." She stepped away from the wall. "Like I always say . . ."

PLUS ON EST DE FOUS, PLUS ON RIT.

"I have no idea what that means."

"It means: the more the merrier," Kate translated.

Beatrice pondered the phrase. She took a deep breath and watched her sister's face. "What about me?" she asked. "Or is that scarier?"

Downstairs a car door slammed. The front door opened and closed. Henry tried out his French while Nancy Zinker cooed her hellos.

Kate raised her eyebrows. "You really want to join my club?"

"Maybe," said Beatrice. "Does Pig Latin count as a language?"

Kate cocked her head to the side, considering. "As a rule—I'd say no."

"That's what I thought," Beatrice said. She wasn't even sure why she'd asked.

Kate took a step toward Beatrice, her face softening. "But I could think about it."

"Maybe you should come up here while you think." Beatrice patted the mattress and scooted over to make room. "I highly recommend it."

Kate laughed and climbed the ladder to join her.

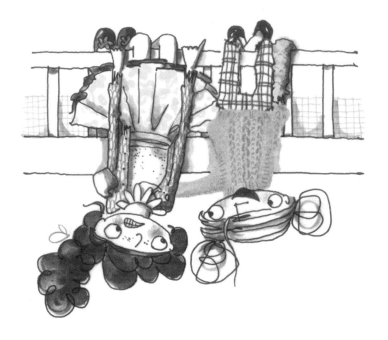

"Whoa," said Kate. "Head rush." She rubbed her temples. "From now on, I'll leave the upside down thinking to you. But this did speed up my decision."

"Wow, that was fast—what's the verdict?"

"I-yay an-cay end-bay e-thay ules-ray or-fay ou-yay."

Beatrice couldn't believe her ears, so she

clarified it, just to be sure. "Did you just say you'd bend the rules for me? In Pig Latin?"

Kate's face turned red. *"Aybe-may,"* she said.

"Girls! We're home!" Nancy Zinker called from the kitchen.

Beatrice flipped to the ground. "So Pig Latin counts?"

"Dinner's ready!" Pete Zinker announced.

"That's what I said," Kate confirmed. "You and your language are in—if you want to be."

Kate struggled to sit up. "A little help here, please?"

Beatrice reached over her head and rotated her sister right side up.

Kate blinked her eyes, struggling to adjust. "You really think better like that?"

"Like magic," Beatrice told her. "Every single time."

Pete and Nancy Zinker were waiting at the bottom of the stairs when Beatrice came down. Funny looks stretched across their faces. Beatrice turned from one to the other. "What's going on?" she asked her mother.

Nancy Zinker smiled at her daughter. "We heard about your day," she told her. "Are you really okay?" She inspected Beatrice's nose while Beatrice nodded her head. Smoothing Beatrice's hair, she said, "Your father had an idea."

Beatrice peeked over their shoulders. The table was set and the good china was out, but the kitchen did not smell like dinner.

Her dad wrapped her in a giant hug. "I thought

we should eat dessert first tonight," he said. "Beatrice-style!"

Nancy Zinker held up a finger and qualified, "Just this once."

WOW!

There was no dinner, but the plates weren't empty.

"*Oh là là*," Kate gasped behind her. "So fancy."

Beatrice dropped into her seat, smiling at her plate. Like Lenny earlier, she didn't know what to say.

"If you aren't going to eat it, I sure will," her dad said. He raised his fork and saluted her. "To Beatrice!"

PINEAPPLE UPSIDE DOWN CAKE

HER FAVORITE

Beatrice scooped up a huge helping and closed her eyes. "Wow," she said.

It was the only word for it.

"Wow indeed," declared her father, digging in. "Almost as good as bacon."

"Kaka!" Henry cheered, smashing a huge handful on his head.

Nancy Zinker clapped her hands together. "He said cake!"

Pete Zinker set down his fork. "He sure did!"

"In Icelandic!" said Kate.

Nancy Zinker rushed for the camera.

"Bon appétit!" Kate shouted as the flash went off.

"Bon appétit!" everyone agreed.

Beatrice wanted to memorize this moment.

Not everything in her life was a piece of cake—but tonight, the Zinkers were eating cake for dinner. And tomorrow, if all went according to plan, Operation Upside would surprise another winner.

All because of a green-glasses-girl and an upside down thinker.

Acknowledgments

Words seem ridiculously inadequate to express my gratitude for all the people who have helped Beatrice meet the world.

Nevertheless:

Endless thanks, exclamation points, and happy tears for my kind and wonderful editor, Rotem Moscovich. Thank you for believing in Beatrice, and for all the ways you spoke into the story and made it better. I am so grateful. Many thanks to Phil Caminiti for the book design, to Greg Pizzoli for sharing his technical knowledge, and to the entire team of amazing people at Disney Hyperion.

To my agent, Stephen Barr—thank you for seeing more in me, and in Beatrice, than I did myself, and for pointing the way with genius, patience, and fun. This book would not exist without you. It's a tremendous gift to experience all the upsides of knowing you.

Thanks to Angharad Kowal, Cecilia de la Campa, Nikoline Nordfred Eriksen, and everyone else at Writers House, for your enthusiasm on Beatrice's behalf.

Thank you to the family and friends who encouraged me along the way. Your support means more than I can say, and I love you all. A special thank-you to my friends at the Target Starbucks who gave me the happiest place to write every day.

To my three favorite people: Bob, Matthew, and Nolan—thanks for being your wonderful selves, and the very best part of my life. "Aren't we lucky?"